by David McPhail

Little, Brown and Company

BOSTON   NEW YORK   TORONTO   LONDON

Books by David McPhail

THE BEAR'S TOOTHACHE

ANDREW'S BATH

HENRY BEAR'S PARK

THE TRAIN

FIRST FLIGHT

SOMETHING SPECIAL

LOST!

THE PARTY

SANTA'S BOOK OF NAMES

Library of Congress Cataloging-in-Publication Data

McPhail, David M.
  The train.

  Summary: During the night while everyone is asleep, a young boy takes a ride on his toy train.
  [1. Railroads–Trains–Fiction] I. Title.
PZ7.M2427Tr   [E]   76-45791
ISBN 0-316-56316-1 (HC)
ISBN 0-316-56331-5 (PB)

          10 9 8 7 6   (HC)
        10 9 8 7 6 5 4   (PB)

              BP

Published simultaneously in Canada
by Little, Brown & Company (Canada) Limited

Printed in the United States of America

For my father, Ben,
who gave me my first train

Matthew loved trains.

Most of all he loved his own train. It was
set up on a table in one corner of the bedroom
that he shared with his baby brother.

The train tracks ran over a bridge,
into a tunnel and out, and through
a small town.
In the town there was a station where the train
could stop to pick up passengers and baggage.

One night, after they were all
washed and ready for bed, Matthew
let his baby brother run the train.

"That's too fast!" said Matthew
to his baby brother. "Slow it down!"

But it was too late. The train went
off the track and fell onto the floor.
CRASH!

Matthew was angry.
His baby brother started to cry.

Matthew just couldn't be angry any longer.
"It's all right," he said, "I can fix it."

Matthew picked up the train
and put it back on the track.

He got his tools out of the toy box
and started to fix it.

"That will have to wait till morning,"
said Matthew's father.
"Right now it's time for bed."

"Can we read a book first?" asked Matthew.
"One book," said Matthew's father.

So they read a book about trains.

Then Matthew's mother and father
tucked Matthew and his brother into bed
and kissed them goodnight.

13

14

"Pleasant dreams," said Matthew's mother
as she put out the light.

Matthew lay in bed for a long time.
He wasn't tired so he decided to get up
and work on the train.

Matthew climbed out of bed very quietly
and turned on the light.

His train stood there waiting on the track.
It made a hissing noise.

The conductor was telling the passengers
that the train was broken.

"I can fix it," said Matthew.
He picked up his tools
and walked over to the engine.

One of the wheels was loose,
so Matthew tightened it with his wrench.

He pounded out some dents
with his hammer and touched up
the scratches with his paint and brush.

Then he cleaned
the headlight,

and helped the stationmaster load the baggage car.

He carried aboard some suitcases.

When the train started to move,
the conductor let Matthew punch tickets.

He sold ice cream, magazines and comic books, and passed out pillows to sleepy passengers.

The train stopped
to take on water,
and the engineer
invited Matthew
to ride with him
in the engine.

Matthew helped the fireman stoke the boiler.

Then he sat with the engineer and drove the train.
"Not too fast," said the engineer.

Matthew slowed the train
and blew the whistle.

He was very tired, so he stopped the train.
The engineer carried him to the sleeping car,
where a berth was all ready for him.

"Pleasant dreams," said the engineer. "Thank
you for fixing the train."
"You're welcome," said Matthew.

"Good night."